P9-CED-613

Desert Baths

by Darcy Pattison

illustrated by Kathleen Rietz

The desert dawn sends light washing over the land. The turkey vulture wakes and turns east, stretching his wings to warm up in a sunbath.

Early-morning water drops glisten here and there, a light scattering of dew. An Anna's hummingbird slides down a leaf, rubbing her breast feathers in the dew, then flies, shaking off the extra water. After her bath, she perches and preens.

The desert tortoise peeks out of his burrow hoping for a late-morning rain. But the skies are clear. No bath today! He retreats from the heat into his shady burrow.

The roadrunner dashes from shade to shade, hiding from the hot, noon sun. He stops in an open spot and scratches the dirt until it's soft and dusty. He dips his breast, flutters his wings, and shuffles his feet, kicking up a cloud of dust. After his dust bath, he shakes and dashes again for shade.

The mule deer doe visits the fawns' bedding area. The twins suckle, then the doe grooms them. The doe moves off to graze, while the fawns doze in the early afternoon heat.

Late-afternoon heat shimmers above the dry ground. A diamondback rattler wiggles, scrapes, twists, and rolls, turning his skin inside out. Now, he's fresh and clean and one size larger. *Rattle!* When he shed his skin, he also added a bead to his rattle. *Rattle!*

Just as the sunset stains the western sky, the scaled quail hops onto to an ant nest. She picks up an ant in her beak and strokes it under her wings and across her side feathers. When she finishes her anointing, or ant bath, she calls, *Pe-cos, pe-cos, pe-cos.*

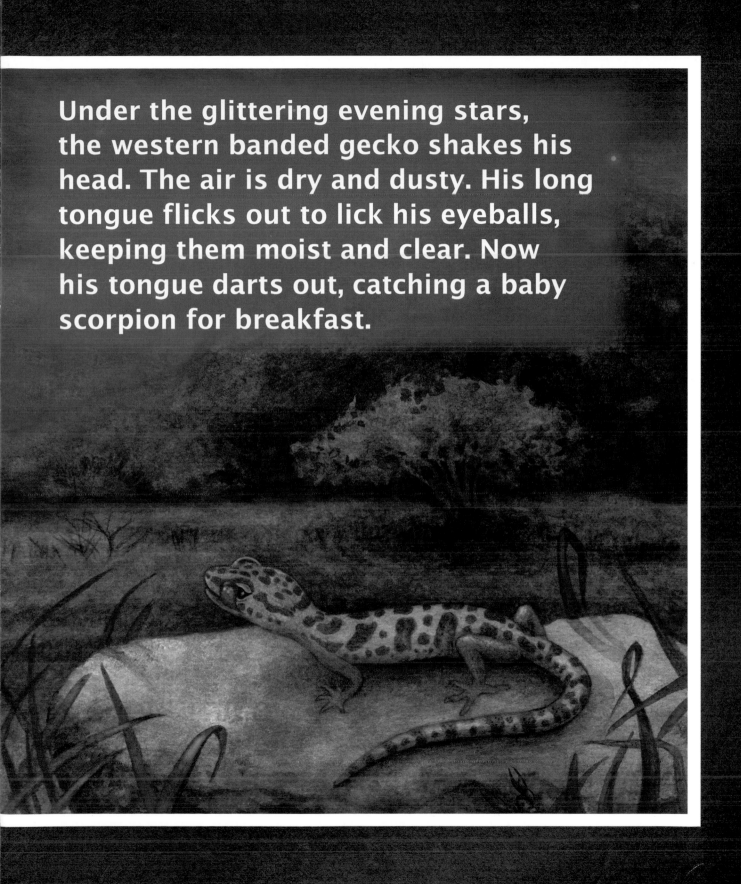

Under the glittering evening stars, the western banded gecko shakes his head. The air is dry and dusty. His long tongue flicks out to lick his eyeballs, keeping them moist and clear. Now his tongue darts out, catching a baby scorpion for breakfast.

The javelina trots to a small seep of water, a place of thick, cool mud. He rolls and scratches and wallows. Then he stands and shakes. It's night—time to forage.

The pallid bat flies low, listening for insects. It dips and snatches a scorpion from the ground. By midnight, he's full and roosts in a crevice. He takes a spit bath, licking his fur. When he is clean and rested, he lurches up and flies to hunt again.

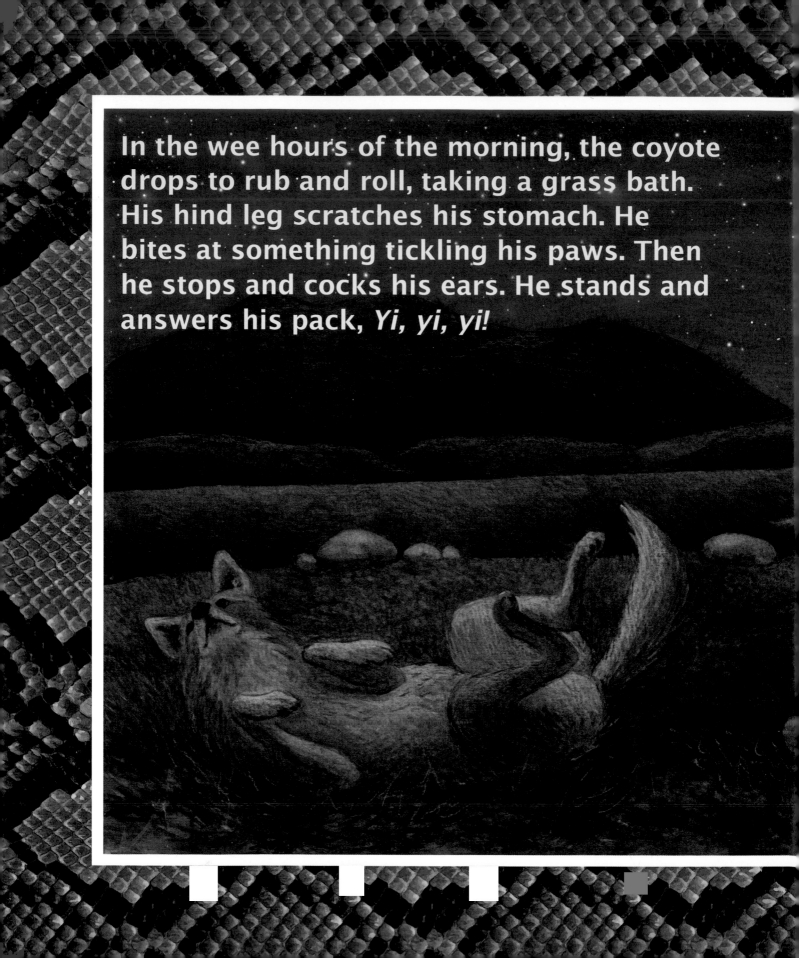

In the wee hours of the morning, the coyote drops to rub and roll, taking a grass bath. His hind leg scratches his stomach. He bites at something tickling his paws. Then he stops and cocks his ears. He stands and answers his pack, *Yi, yi, yi!*

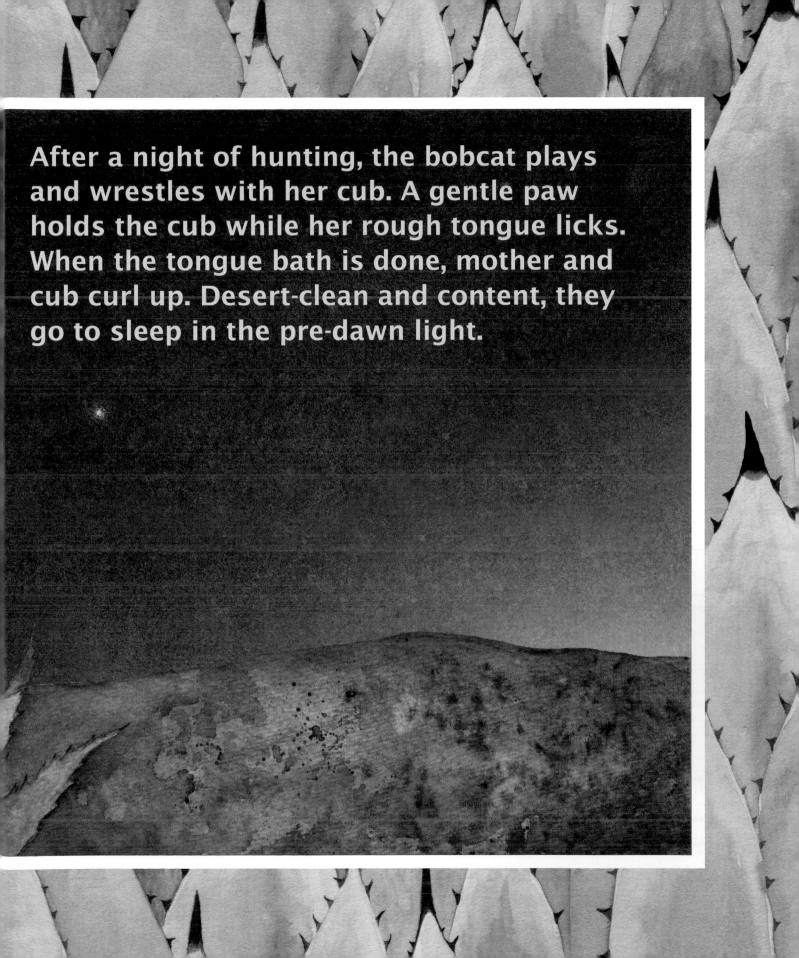

After a night of hunting, the bobcat plays and wrestles with her cub. A gentle paw holds the cub while her rough tongue licks. When the tongue bath is done, mother and cub curl up. Desert-clean and content, they go to sleep in the pre-dawn light.

For Creative Minds

Desert Habitat Fun Facts

A habitat is where something lives—where it can meet all of its basic needs. Living things interact with each other and the non-living things in that same habitat. There are many different types of habitats all over the world.

Living things rely on non-living things in their habitat: soil, water, air, and climate.

Plants need water, nutrients, sunlight and heat in which to grow, and a way for seeds to move (disperse).

Animals need food, water, oxygen to breathe, and a safe space for shelter and for giving birth to their young.

Some deserts are hot and some are cold, but all deserts have a dry climate. Deserts receive an average of less than 10 to 12 inches (25 to 30 cm) of rain per year! Parts of the Atacama Desert in South America haven't had any rain in 100 years. The deserts of the American Southwest average between 2 to 8 inches of rain a year.

Desert plants and animals must survive with little water.

In some ways, clouds act like a blanket at night. Thick, heavy clouds help keep warm temperatures on land. When there are no clouds at night, the land loses all the heat from the sun that had built up all day. Because deserts are so dry, they don't have many clouds. Deserts that get very hot during the day can get very cold at night.

Plants and animals that live in hot deserts have to be able to stay cool during the day but warm at night.

Some cactuses need specific types of bats to pollinate them. Because bats are active at night (nocturnal), these cactuses bloom at night to attract the bats!

There are deserts all over the world—even in the Arctic and Antarctic!

Desert Adaptations Matching

bobcats   coyotes   desert tortoises   javelinas   mule deer

bats   rattlesnakes   roadrunners   scaled quails   turkey vultures

Match the desert animal to the adaptation that allows it to survive in the dry desert.

1. These reptiles store up to a quart of water in their bladders and can go weeks without eating or drinking. They also dig burrows to hide from the heat during the day and dig holes to catch rain when it does fall.

2. These birds soar without flapping their wings often so they don't use up energy while on long searches for food.

3. These flying mammals sleep in crevices in canyon walls or deep in caves where it's cooler.

4. These (two) mammals hunt at night when it's cooler.

5. These reptiles go into the burrows of other animals or under brush to cool off in the heat.

6. These mammals are active around dusk and dawn in the colder months and at night during the hottest months. They can get water from eating their favorite food: the prickly pear cactus.

7. These mammals will eat a wide variety of vegetation to get all the nutrients that they need. During hot seasons, they are active at night and in the cooler morning hours.

8. These birds prefer running to flying. While they will drink water, they usually get enough water from the small animals they eat.

9. These birds prefer running to flying too. Large social groups roost together for warmth on cold nights.

Answers: 1) desert tortoises, 2) turkey vultures, 3) bats, 4) coyotes and bobcats, 5) diamondback rattlesnakes, 6) javelina, 7) mule deer, 8) roadrunner, 9) scaled quail

Deserts in North America

1 Which two deserts are in both the United States and Mexico?

2 Which desert is in part of Texas?

3 Which desert is in part of Oregon?

4 In what two states is the Sonoran Desert?

5 The turkey vulture can be found in every U.S. state except Alaska and Hawaii. In which deserts can you find the turkey vulture?

6 Are there any deserts in the state or province in which you live?

7 If not, what states would you have to go through to get to the closest desert?

Bath Time: True or False

Which statements are true or false?

1. Not all animals use water to bathe.

2. Animals take baths to get rid of dirt, germs, bugs, and parasites.

3. Humans use soap and water in their baths to get rid of dirt and germs.

4. Javelinas roll around in mud to cool off and to scrape off parasites.

5. Some animals (cats, dogs, bats) lick themselves to get clean.

6. Scaled quail put ants on their feathers. As the ants move, they drop an acid that helps protect the birds' skin.

7. Western banded geckos don't have eyelids. They lick their eyeballs to keep them moist and clean.

8. Roadrunners take dust baths. The dust clogs the breathing holes of the parasites in the feathers. Then, when the birds shake off the dust, the parasites drop off too.

9. Desert tortoises go out whenever it rains to drink water and soak in puddles.

10. Snakes shed their small, dirty skin a few times a year. The new skin is big, healthy, and clean.

11. Turkey vultures spread their wings in the sunlight to maintain body temperature and feather health. Sunning makes parasites move to other parts of the bird's feathers, making it easier for the birds to remove them (preening).

Food For Thought

Personal hygiene means the ways you stay clean.

How do you wash your hands?

How do you clean your teeth?

How do you take a bath?

How often do you take a bath?

How is your personal hygiene similar to or different from the animals' personal hygiene?

Answers: All are true!

What Time of Day?

Throughout history and all over the world, people do certain things at certain times of the day. We do too. We brush our teeth and eat breakfast when we get up in the morning. We usually eat lunch around noon and dinner or supper in the evening. Some people take showers or baths in the evening and some take them in the morning.

All over the world, with the exception of the Arctic and Antarctic, the sun rises in the east early in the morning, is high in the sky midday, and then sets in the west in the evening. You can tell if it is morning or afternoon by where the sun is in the sky.

The moon rises in the east and sets in the west but rises and sets at a different time each day. Depending on where it is in the moon (lunar) cycle, the shape looks different too!

1  Can you tell what time of day it is by where the sun is? Is it morning (AM) or evening (PM)?

2  The roadrunner runs at noon. What are some things that you might do around noon?

3  Can you tell what time of day it is by where the sun is now?

4  The gecko eats its breakfast in the evening. What meal do you eat in the evening?

5  The pallid bat is up at midnight. What are you doing at midnight?

Answers: 1) Sun rising in the east means it's morning (am). 2) Most people eat lunch around noon. 3) Sun setting in the west means it's evening. 4) Most people eat dinner or supper and many people take baths in the evening. 5) Hopefully you are sleeping!

Hands on: Telling Time by the Sun's Position

Long before people had watches, clocks, or cell phones, they used the sun's position in the sky to tell the time of day. At first, people probably divided the day between sunlight and darkness. Then they probably noticed and watched how the sun moved across the sky and how the shadows changed as the sun moved.

- Go outside early in the morning and notice where the sun is rising—that's east. Turn so the sun is on your right. You are now looking north. Make a drawing of your location showing the sun in the east as if you are looking north.
- Set an alarm or timer and go outside every one or two hours during the day. Make note of the sun's position in the sky. Each time you go outside, add a sun to your drawing to show its location. Make sure to label the time.
- Each time you go outside, look at your shadow or the shadow of things around you. How do the shadows change during the day?
- Each time you look for the sun, check to see if you can see the moon too. If so, where is it and what does it look like?
- Watch to see where the sun sets in the west.

Sundials were the first "clocks." The early sundials were probably little more than a stick in the middle of a circle with notches to show how the shadows moved—based on how the sun moved.

Design and make your own sundial.

What will you use to make your circle?

What will you use for your stick and how will you make it stand up?

What will you use to make your notches to mark the time?

How often will you check your sundial and make notches to show time passage?

Where will you build or place your sundial? It needs to be in a large, sunny spot.

For Zeke—DP

For my brother, Patrick—KR

Thanks to Sid Slone, Refuge Manger, and Margot Bissell, Public Use Assistant at Cabeza Prieta National Wildlife Refuge for verifying the desert habitat information and to the following animal experts for verifying the specific animal bath information: Dr. Donald R. Powers, Professor of Biology at George Fox University—Anna's hummingbirds; Paul J. Weldon, Research Associate, Smithsonian's National Zoological Park—scaled quail; Renee Lizotte, Herpetology Department at the Arizona-Sonora Desert Museum—desert tortoises; and Sue Barnard, Founder of Basically Bats Wildlife Conservation Society and author of *Bats In Captivity*—pallid bats.

Library of Congress Cataloging-in-Publication Data

Pattison, Darcy.

Desert baths / by Darcy Pattison ; illustrated by Kathleen Rietz.

p. cm.

ISBN 978-1-60718-525-3 (hardcover) -- ISBN 978-1-60718-534-5 (pbk.) -- ISBN 978-1-60718-543-7 (English ebook) -- ISBN 978-1-60718-552-9 (Spanish ebook) 1. Desert animals--Juvenile literature. 2. Desert animals--Habitat--Juvenile literature. 3. Baths--Juvenile literature. I. Rietz, Kathleen, ill. II. Title.

QL116.P37 2012

591.754--dc23

2012004377

Also available as eBooks featuring auto-flip, auto-read, 3D-page-curling, and selectable English and Spanish text and audio (ISBN: 978-1-60718-562-8).

Spanish translation (Las duchas en el desierto) hardcover ISBN: 978-1-60718-676-2

Interest level: 004-008   Lexile Level: 870L, Lexile Code: AD

key concepts for educators: desert habitat, animal behavior (adaptations), hygiene, sun & moon patterns in the sky, time of day, differences between day and night, geography (deserts in the US)

Manufactured in China, June, 2012
This product conforms to CPSIA 2008
First Printing

Sylvan Dell Publishing
Mt. Pleasant, SC 29464